THIS WALKER BOOK BELONGS TO:

_____

_____

_____

_____

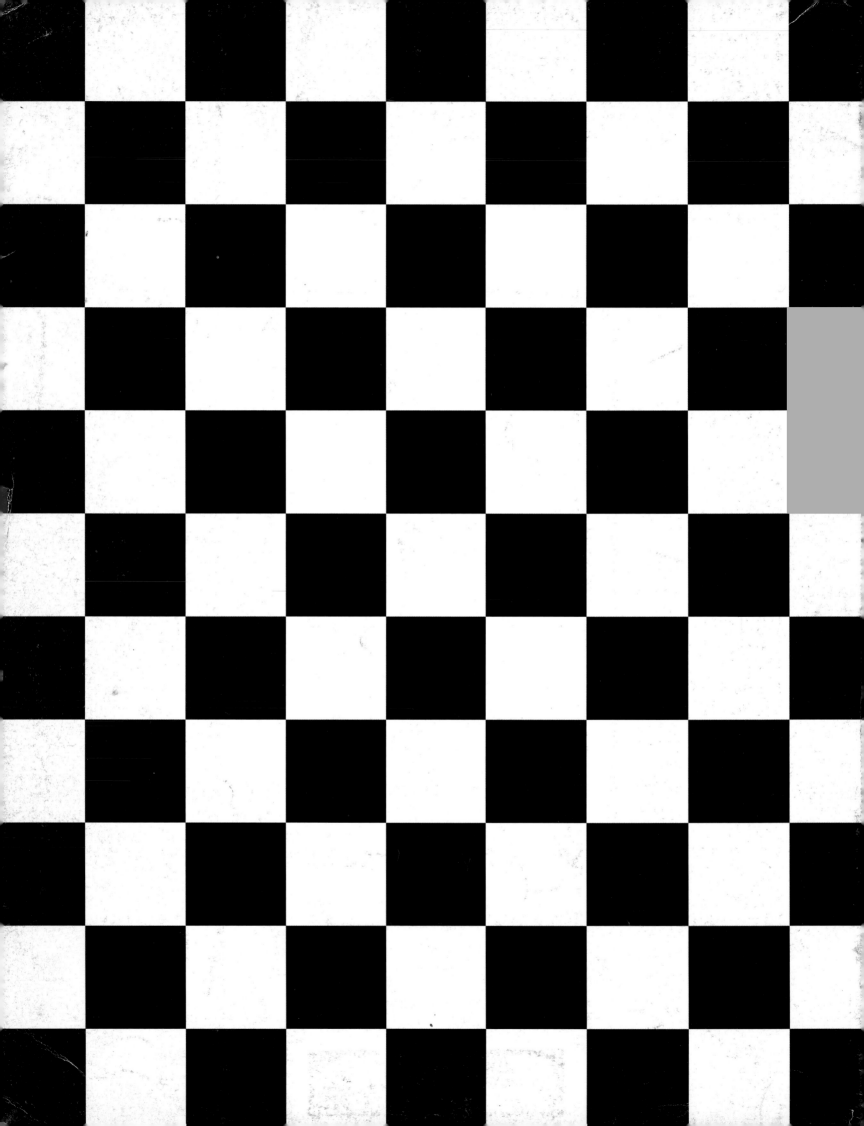

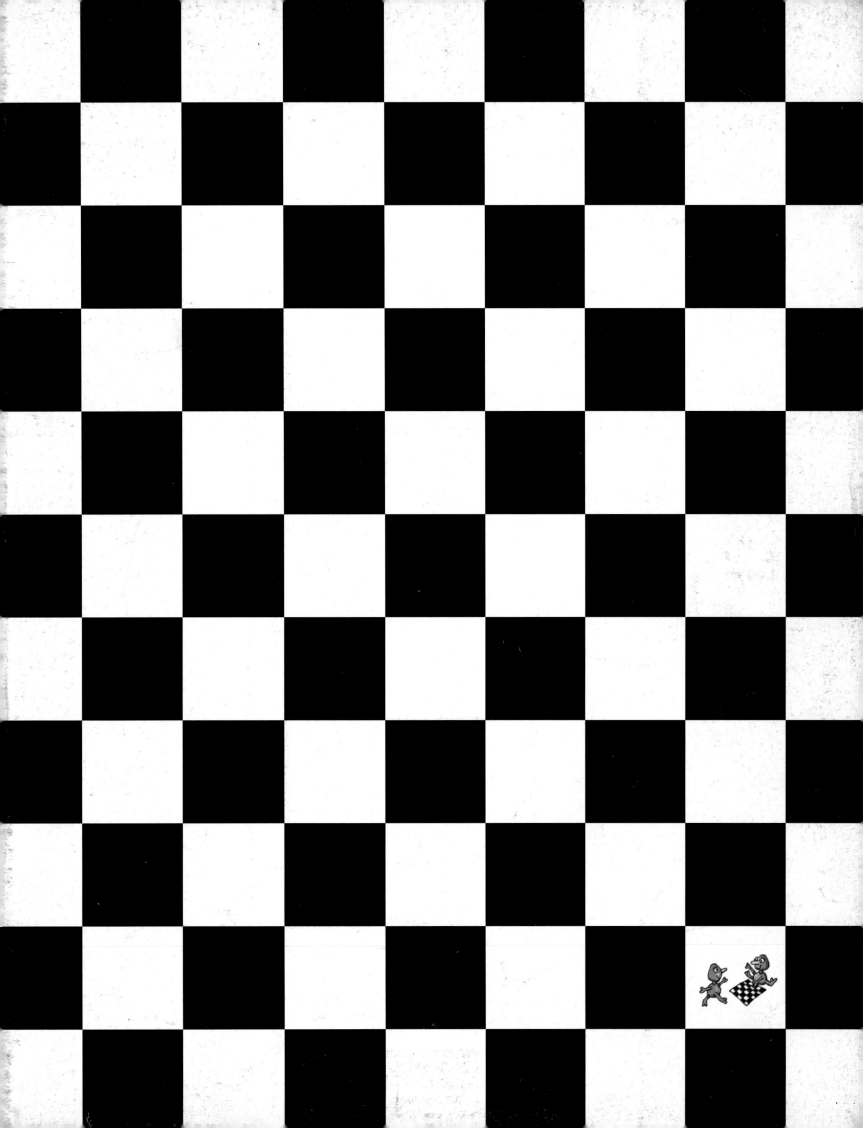

KNIGHT

BISHOP

ROOK

KING

QUEEN

PAWN

To Iain - P.H.

First published 2000 by Walker Books Ltd
87 Vauxhall Walk, London SE11 5HJ

This edition published 2001

2 4 6 8 10 9 7 5 3 1

© 2000 Piers Harper

Printed in Hong Kong

British Library Cataloguing in Publication Data
A catalogue record for this book is
available from the British Library.

ISBN 0-7445-7861-2

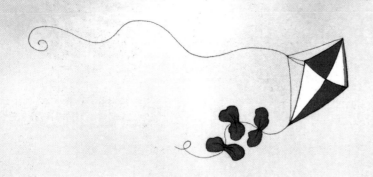

CHECKMATE AT
CHESS CITY

Piers Harper

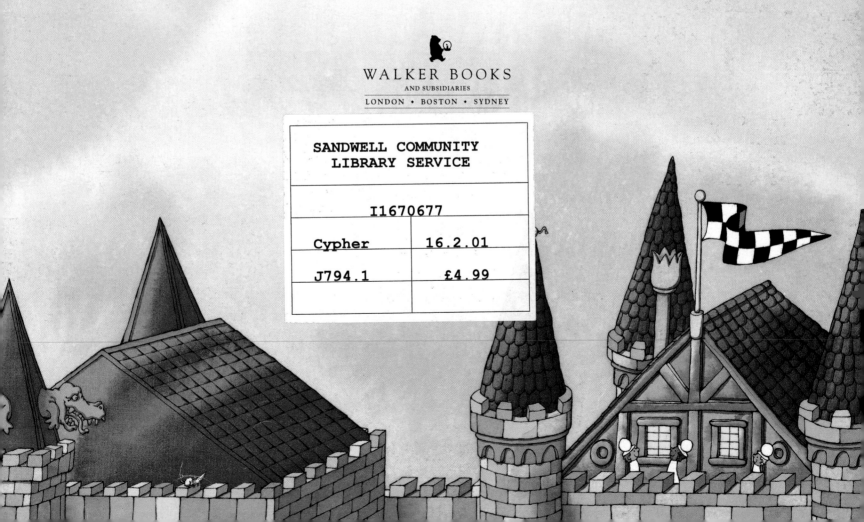

WALKER BOOKS
AND SUBSIDIARIES
LONDON · BOSTON · SYDNEY

CHESS CITY HAS BEEN CAPTURED
BY AN ARMY OF WHITE CHESSMEN!

The Black Chess King and Black Chess Queen
are prisoners in the dungeon of their own castle.
Now the Black Chessmen are marching towards
the city to rescue their rulers. You must help the
Black Pawns and Knights, Bishops and
Rooks to reach Chess City.

The eight Black Pawns are in the desert. Check to see how pawns move, then help them find a route across. You can move one square diagonally if it gets you to a pool of water for a drink. Start again if you touch a cactus.

HOW PAWNS MOVE

Pawns can go two squares straight ahead on their first move and thereafter only one square. Pawns never move backwards or sideways and can only move diagonally to take another chess piece.

FINISH FINISH FINISH FINISH

START START START START

FINISH FINISH FINISH FINISH

START START START START

Help each of the Black Knights find a route across the swamp by jumping from mound to mound.

HOW KNIGHTS MOVE

Knights can only move in an "L" shape made of four squares, including the square they start on (the "L" can point in any direction). They are the only pieces that are allowed to jump over things.

FINISH

START

FINISH

START

Help the Black Bishops across the river to Chess City. Check to see how bishops move, then guide them from bush to bush. When you reach a bush, change direction if you want to. Avoid the hungry wolves!

HOW BISHOPS MOVE

Bishops can move backwards or forwards any number of squares – but they can only go diagonally.

FINISH

START

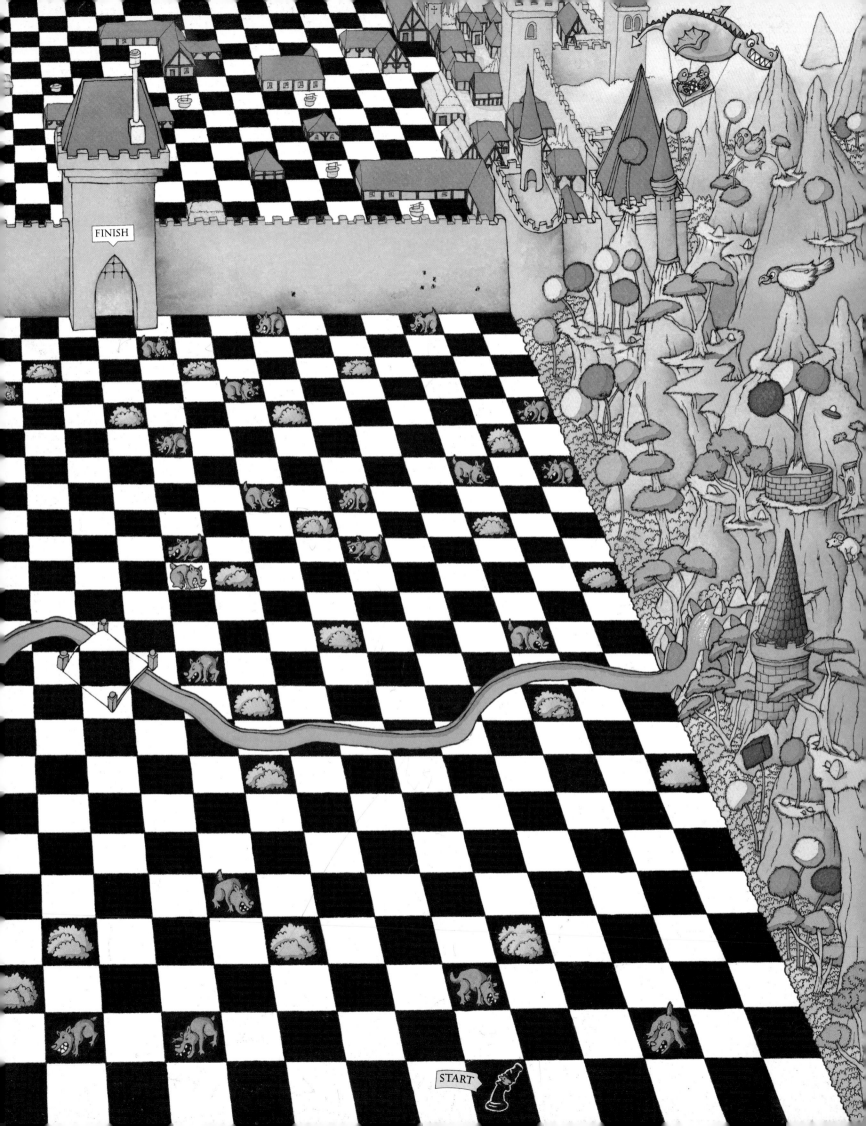

FINISH

START

Help both Black Rooks climb the city wall. Check how rooks move and then guide them from ledge to ledge. When you reach a ledge, change direction if you want to. Don't touch the poisonous spiders!

HOW ROOKS MOVE

Rooks can move any number of squares backwards, forwards or sideways in a straight line, but they cannot move diagonally.

FINIS

START

The Black Pawns have reached the castle walls but the only way into Chess City is via the sewers. Help them find the route through the sewers, collecting exactly eight keys on the way. You can move one square diagonally if it gets you to a square with a key. Start again if you meet a rat!

HOW PAWNS MOVE

Pawns can go two squares straight ahead on their first move and thereafter only one square. Pawns never move backwards or sideways and can only move diagonally to take another chess piece.

START

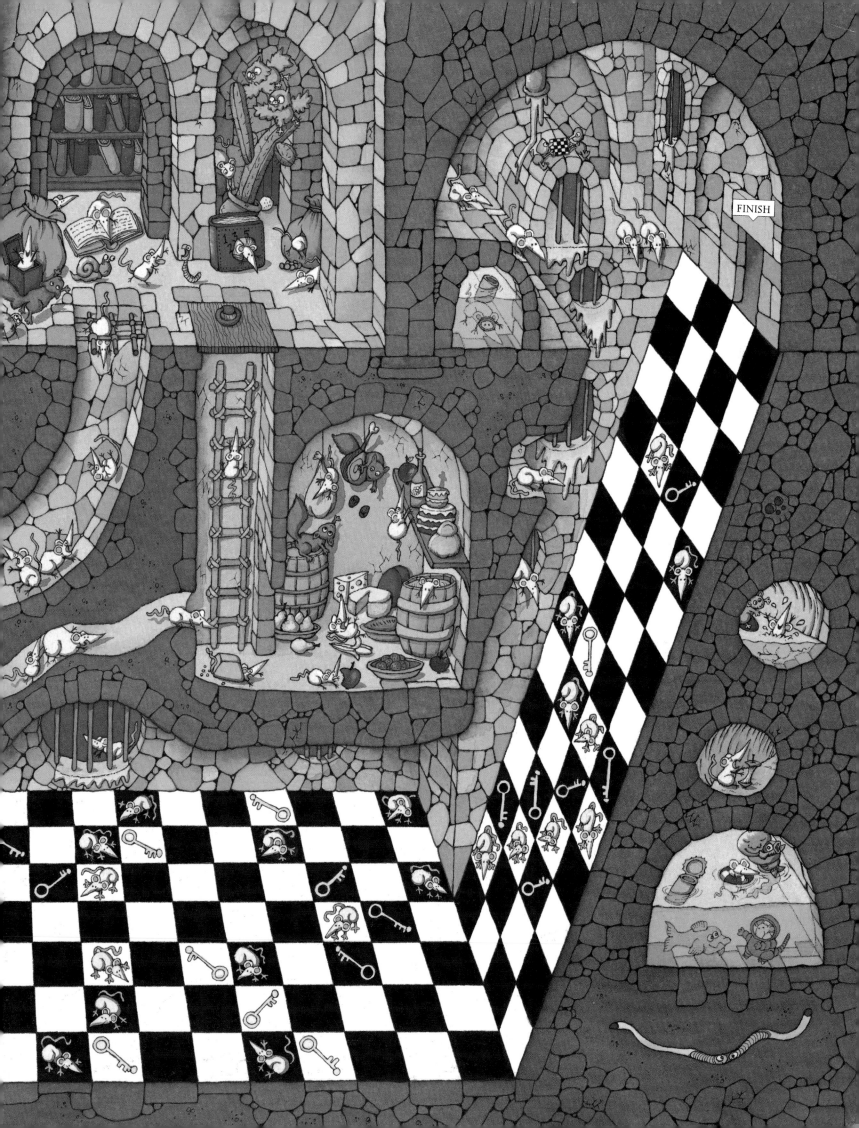

FINISH

Both Black Knights have entered Chess City. Now you must get them across the courtyard and into the castle. Jump from square to square but don't land on any that have cracks.

HOW KNIGHTS MOVE

Knights can only move in an "L" shape made of four squares, including the square they start on (the "L" can point in any direction). They are the only pieces that are allowed to jump over things.

FINISH

START

FINISH

START

The Black Bishops have entered Chess City too! Lead them across the city square by moving from well to well. When you reach a well, change direction if you want to.

HOW BISHOPS MOVE

Bishops can move backwards or forwards any number of squares – but they can only go diagonally.

FINISH

START

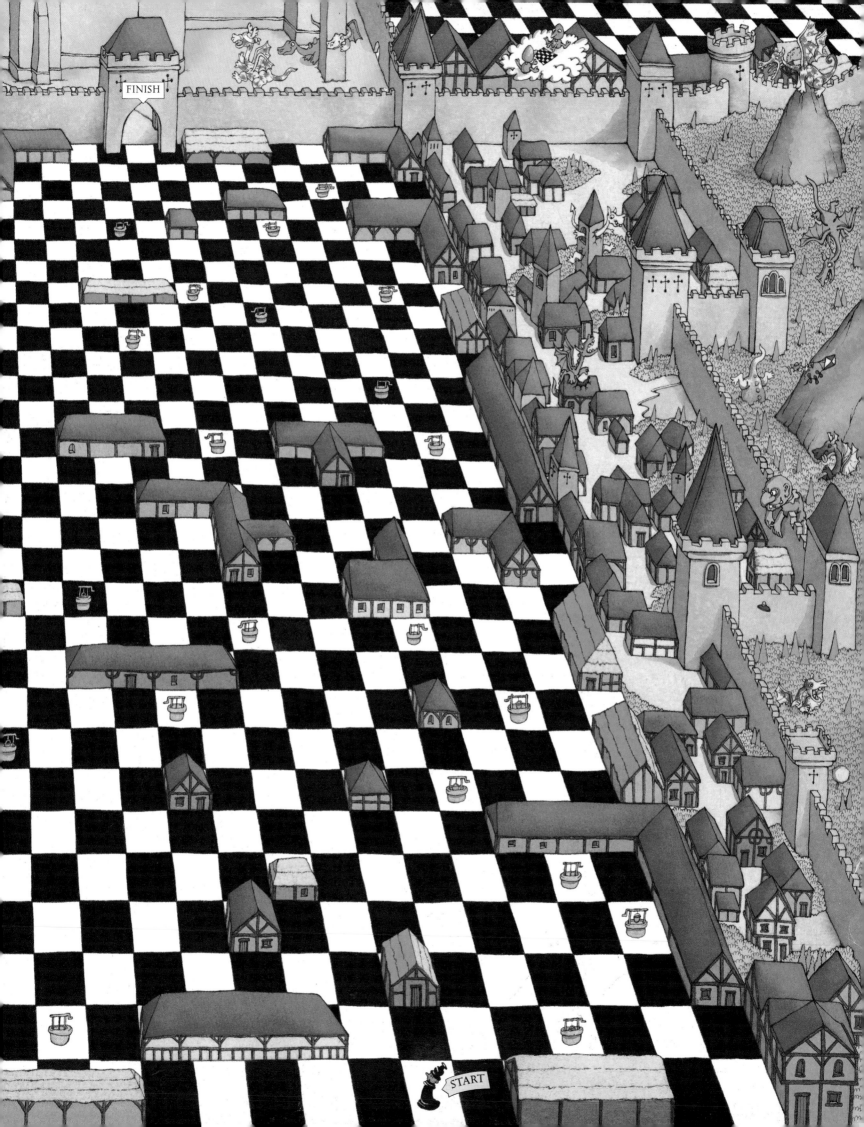

Both Black Rooks are inside Chess City. Can you help them climb across the roof? When you reach a leaf, change direction if you want to. Don't wake the cats – they will raise the alarm.

HOW ROOKS MOVE

Rooks can move any number of squares backwards, forwards or sideways in a straight line, but they cannot move diagonally.

START

START

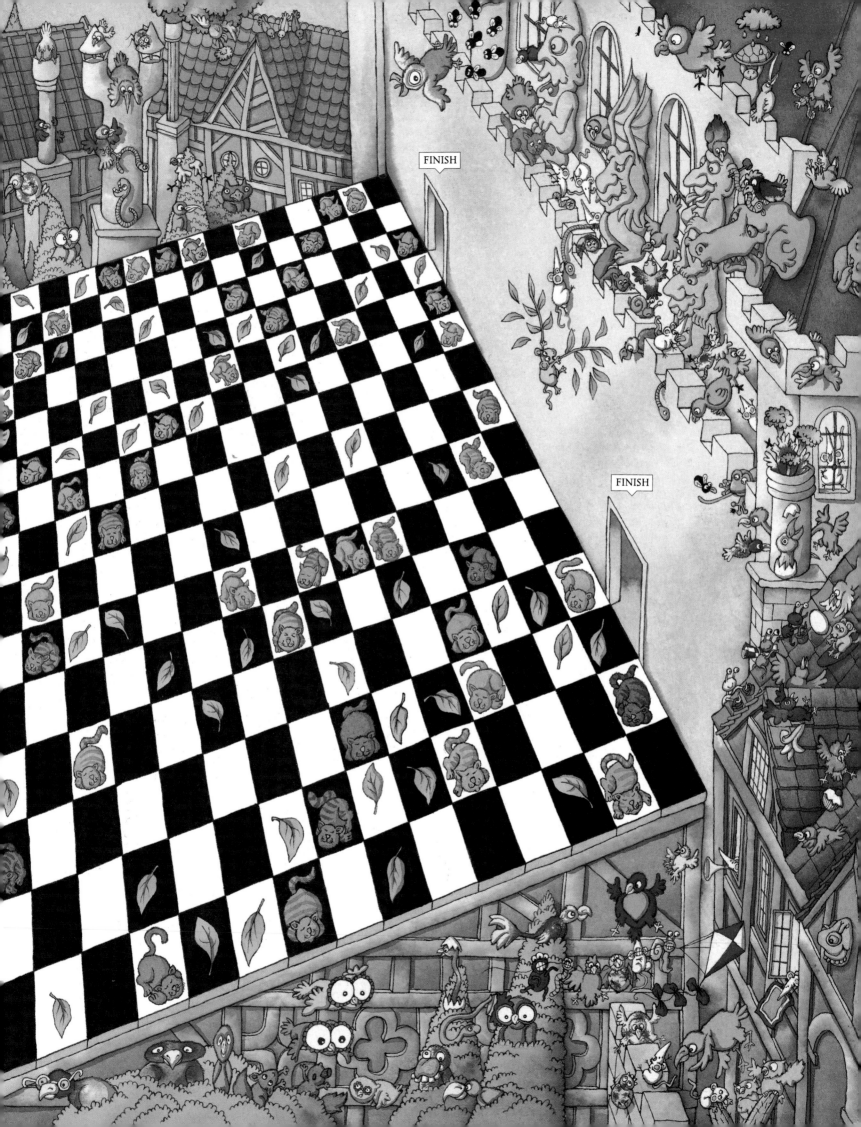

FINISH

FINISH

The Black Pawns and Bishops have crept into the hall of the castle, which is full of maces and swords. Each Pawn must collect five maces and then lock them in one of the cupboards. The Pawns can move one square diagonally in order to get to a mace. The Bishops must collect five swords, and take them to throw out of a window. The Bishops can choose to change direction when they land on a sword. Don't tread on any trapdoors.

The Black Knights have sneaked into the castle dungeon. One Knight must rescue the Black King and the other must rescue the Black Queen. Jump from square to square and don't land on the wooden stakes!

The two Black Rooks have entered the banqueting hall and found all the White Chessmen asleep after celebrating their victory. Each Rook must capture exactly seven of the white pieces on one route and lock them up behind one of the iron doors. Can you help? When you capture a white piece, change direction if you want to. Give it your best shot!

FINISH

FINISH

START

START

The Black King and Queen are free! The White King and Queen, trying to escape, have dropped some scrolls and stolen jewels. The Black King must move from scroll to scroll and capture the White King. The Black Queen must move from jewel to jewel and capture the White Queen. Can you help them both? Remember to avoid the trapdoors on the floor.

HOW KINGS MOVE

A king can move in any direction but can only move one square at a time.

HOW QUEENS MOVE

A queen can move in any direction in a straight line, and any number of squares.

FINISH

FINISH

KING'S START

QUEEN'S START

CONGRATULATIONS!

YOU HAVE HELPED THE
BLACK CHESSMEN DEFEAT THE
WHITE CHESSMEN AND HAVE
FREED CHESS CITY.

THE GAME OF CHESS

Now you know how the different chessmen move, but there is much more to the game.

Chess is like a battle. The white pieces always start the game by moving first, and from then on the players take turns. The players fight by capturing each other's chessmen and taking them off the board. A piece is captured when an enemy piece lands on the same square as it. If you are able to take your opponent's king on your next move, the king is said to be in "check". If your opponent can move the king to a safe spot on the board or can move another piece to protect the king, they do so and the game goes on. If your opponent cannot protect the king or move him out of the way, this is called "checkmate". When this happens the game is over and you have won.

HOW A CHESSBOARD IS SET UP

A chessboard has 64 black and white squares. When you play the game you must position the board so a white square is in the right-hand corner that faces you. Each set of chessmen starts the game in two rows. The row closest to you has a rook (also known as a castle) on each of the far ends, next knights, then bishops, and in the centre the king and queen. The queen always stands on her own colour – the white queen stands on a white square and the black queen on a black square. The eight pawns stand in front.

There are other special rules but the best way of learning them is to play chess with someone who can already play. Every game of chess is different and the game is well worth learning.

HOW PAWNS MOVE

Pawns can go two squares straight ahead on their first move and thereafter only one square. Pawns never move backwards or sideways and can only move diagonally to take another chess piece.

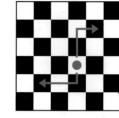

HOW KNIGHTS MOVE

Knights can only move in an "L" shape made of four squares, including the square they start on (the "L" can point in any direction). They are the only pieces that are allowed to jump over things.

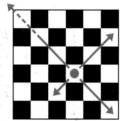

HOW BISHOPS MOVE

Bishops can move backwards or forwards any number of squares – but they can only go diagonally.

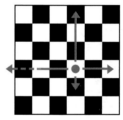

HOW ROOKS MOVE

Rooks can move any number of squares backwards, forwards or sideways in a straight line, but they cannot move diagonally.

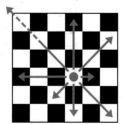

HOW QUEENS MOVE

A queen can move in any direction in a straight line, and any number of squares.

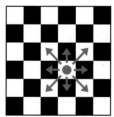

HOW KINGS MOVE

A king can move in any direction but can only move one square at a time.

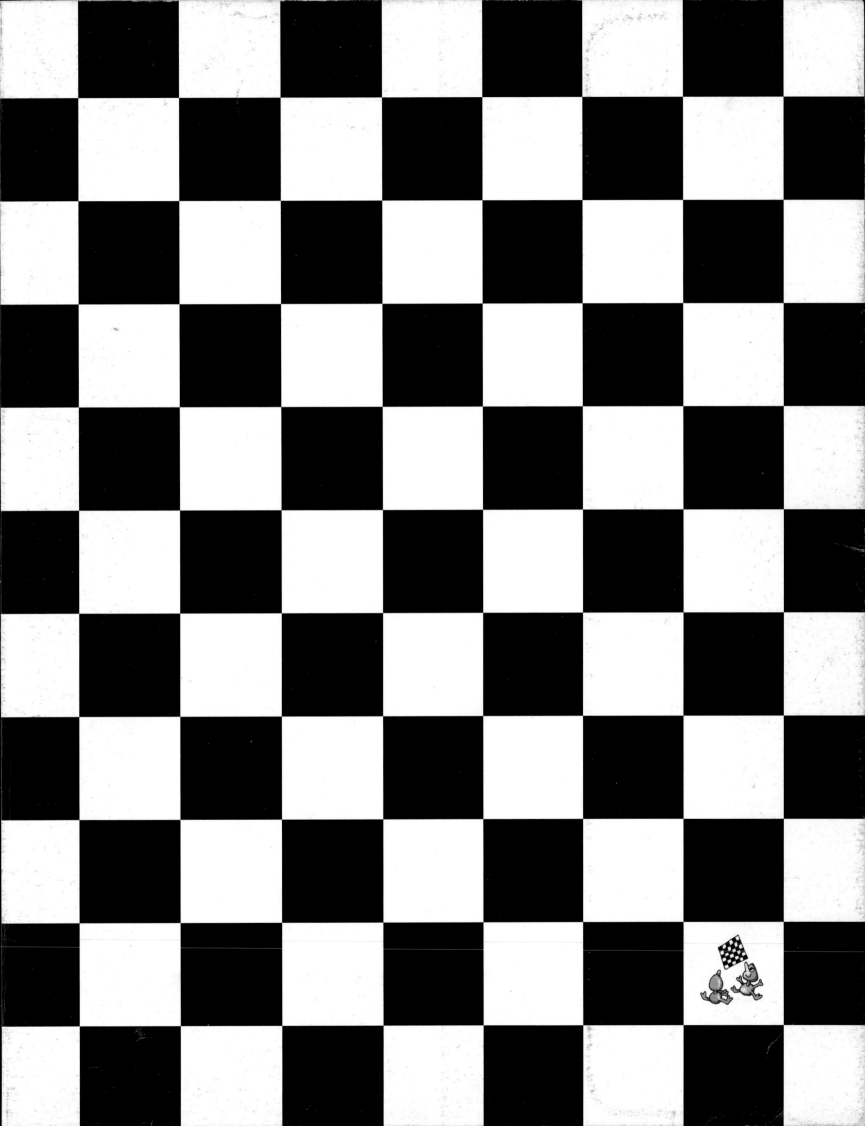

PIERS HARPER got the idea for **Checkmate at Chess City** whilst sitting in a caravan on holiday. "It was pouring down with rain," he says, "and there was nothing to do except play chess – which I hadn't done since I was about ten years old. As I tried to remember the moves of each of the pieces it occurred to me how difficult I'd found it initially to learn them, but that a puzzle book might be a fun way of doing it."

Piers Harper studied Ancient History and Classical Civilizations at Sheffield University. A self-taught artist, he has illustrated a number of children's books, including *Snakes and Ladders* (*and Hundreds of Mice!*), *If You Love a Bear* and *Turtle Quest*. He has worked in a children's bookshop and as a youth worker. He lives in Cumbria.

Some more Walker game books

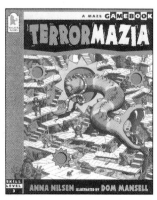

ISBN 0-7445-4708-3 (pb)

ISBN 0-7445-6083-7 (pb)

ISBN 0-7445-6350-X (pb)

ISBN 0-7445-6349-6 (pb)